MIDLOTHIAN LIBRARY SERVICE

Please return/renew this item by the last date shown. To
renew please give your borrower number. Renewal may
be made in person, online, or by post, e-mail or phone.
www.midlothian.gov.uk/library

This Book Belongs To

. . . .

First published in 2000
by Hodder Children's Books

A Catalogue record for this book is available from the
British Library

ISBN 0 340 77935 7

Printed and bound in Great Britain
by Omnia Books Ltd, Glasgow

Hodder Children's Books
A Division of Hodder Headline Limited
338 Euston Road, London NW1 3BH

Smiler Gets Toothache

Written by Margaret Ryan

Illustrated by David Melling

Hodder
Children's
Books

a division of Hodder Headline Limited

To Bob
with love -
Margaret Ryan

For Daniel, Niall and Katherine -
David Melling

Smiler, the crocodile,
had toothache.

He had
toothache
when he ate.

He had
toothache
when he
drank.

He even had
toothache
when he smiled.

"This toothache is really sore,"
he groaned.
"OOH . . . AAH . . . OOH."

He waddled out of the river on to
the bank and groaned again.
"OOH . . . AAH . . . OOH."

Up in the trees, Bumpy,
the sun bear, heard the noise.
She bumped down on to the
riverbank to find out what
was wrong.

"What's the matter, Smiler?" she said. "Have you got tummy-ache? I often get tummy-ache when I've eaten too much honey."

"No," groaned
Smiler. "It's not
tummy-ache.
Crocodiles don't
eat too much. It's
toothache. Look in my
mouth, Bumpy. See if you can
find the sore tooth."

Bumpy looked in Smiler's mouth.
There were lots of big teeth
in there.

She put her
paw in and
wiggled a
front one.
It was all
right. It
didn't hurt.

She put her
paw in and
wiggled a
back one.
It was all
right.
It didn't
hurt either.

She put her paw in and wiggled
two more teeth. But she couldn't
find the sore one.

"You are so lazy, Smiler," said Bumpy. "Don't you ever clean your teeth? I can see last week's dinner on them."
But Smiler just groaned again. Louder still.
"OOH . . . AAH . . . OOH."

Up in the trees, Rainbow, the parrot, heard the noise. She flew down to the riverbank to find out what was wrong.

"What's the matter, Smiler?" she said. "Have you got beak-ache? I often get beak-ache when I've been talking too much."

"No," groaned Smiler. "I haven't
got a beak, you silly bird. And
crocodiles don't talk too much.
It's toothache. Look in my
mouth, Rainbow. See if you can
find the sore tooth."

Rainbow looked in Smiler's mouth. There were lots of big teeth in there.

She put her beak in and wiggled a front one. It was all right. It didn't hurt.

She put her beak in and wiggled a back one. It was all right. It didn't hurt either.

She put her beak in and wiggled
three more teeth. But she
couldn't find the sore one.

"You are so lazy, Smiler," she said. "Don't you ever clean your teeth? I can see last month's dinner on them."
But Smiler just groaned again. Even louder. "OOH . . . AAH . . . OOH."

Up in the trees, Fuzzbuzz, the little orang-utan, heard the noise. He swung down to the riverbank to find out what was wrong.

"What's the matter, Smiler?" he said. "Have you got arm-ache? I often get arm-ache when I've been swinging too much from the trees."

"No," groaned Smiler. "It's not arm-ache. Crocodiles don't swing from the trees. It's toothache. Look in my mouth, Fuzzbuzz. See if you can find the sore tooth."

Fuzzbuzz looked in Smiler's mouth. There were lots of big teeth in there.

He put his hand in and wiggled a front one. It was all right. It didn't hurt.

He put his hand in and wiggled a back one. It was all right. It didn't hurt either.

He put his hand in and wiggled
four more teeth. But he couldn't
find the sore one.

"You are so lazy, Smiler," he said.
"Don't you ever clean your teeth?
I can see last year's dinner
on them."

Fuzzbuzz put his hand back into
Smiler's mouth and was just
wiggling another big tooth
right at the back when they
heard a noise . . .

**"WE'RE LEAN, WE'RE MEAN,
WE'RE VERY VERY KEEN
TO STING ANY BIT OF YOU
THAT CAN BE SEEN!"**

And marching out of the bat
cave came . . .

"The Angry Ant Gang," cried
Smiler. "Well, they're not
stinging me. I'm going
back down to the river."

And he shut his mouth with a
loud **SNAP**.

"Ow," yelled Fuzzbuzz, and got his hand out just in time.

"OOH . . . AAH." Smiler began to groan again, then he stopped.

"That's funny," he said.
"My toothache's gone away."
"That's because I've got your sore tooth," grinned Fuzzbuzz.

"Look. When I pulled out my hand I pulled out your sore tooth, too."

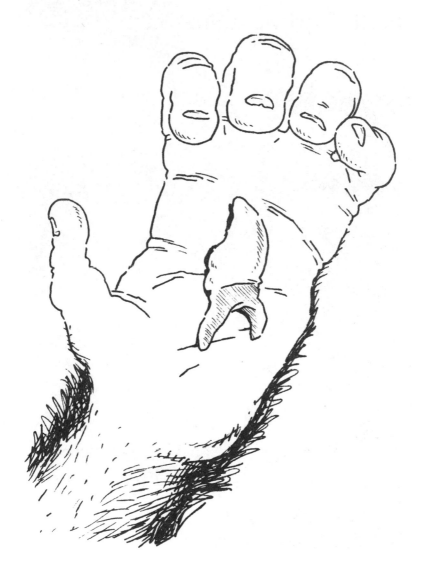

"Well done, Fuzzbuzz," grinned
Smiler. "That feels much better."
And he waddled quickly back
down into the river.

Fuzzbuzz climbed quickly to the top of his tree. "You will remember to clean your teeth now, Smiler, won't you?" he called.

"Oh yes," said Smiler. "I'll remember."

Rainbow flew quickly to the
top of her tree.
"You won't forget, Smiler,
will you?" she called.

"Oh no," said Smiler.
"I won't forget."

Bumpy climbed quickly to the
top of her tree.
"Do you promise, Smiler?"
she called.

"I promise," said Smiler.

Then they all grinned as the Angry Ant Gang marched past muttering . . .

"YOU GOT AWAY THIS TIME,
BUT WE WILL BE BACK.
WE'LL GET YOU NEXT TIME
WE FEEL LIKE A SNACK!"

Next day the jungle friends went down to the river.
"We'll see if Smiler has cleaned his teeth yet," they said.

They found Smiler snoozing in
the sun on the riverbank.

"Have you cleaned last week's dinner off your teeth yet, Smiler?" asked Bumpy.

"Sort of," grinned Smiler.

"Have you cleaned last month's dinner off your teeth yet, Smiler?" asked Rainbow.

"In a way,"
grinned Smiler.

"Have you
cleaned last
year's dinner
off your teeth
yet, Smiler?"
asked Fuzzbuzz.

"Nearly,"
grinned Smiler.

Then he opened his mouth wide
and all the little jungle birds
hopped in and out, in and out.

They pecked
the food
from Smiler's
front teeth.
PECK PECK
PECK.

They pecked
the food
from
Smiler's back
teeth. PECK
PECK PECK.

They peck peck pecked the food
from all the rest of Smiler's teeth.

The jungle friends watched in amazement.

Smiler grinned. "This is how lazy crocodiles clean their teeth," he said.

Look out for more adventures with the

Written by Margaret Ryan
Illustrated by David Melling

Rainbow to the Rescue

Rainbow the parrot talks so much, she drives her friends mad. But when she disappears, they miss her chatter. How can they make her come back?

Fuzzbuzz Takes a Tumble

Fuzzbuzz the orang-utan is fed up. No one will play with him, and there isn't anywhere safe to sleep. What will Fuzzbuzz do when night-time comes?

Bumpy's Rumbling Tummy

Bumpy the sun bear is busy finding food to fill her rumbling tummy. She ignores her friends — but will she spot the Angry Ant gang in time?